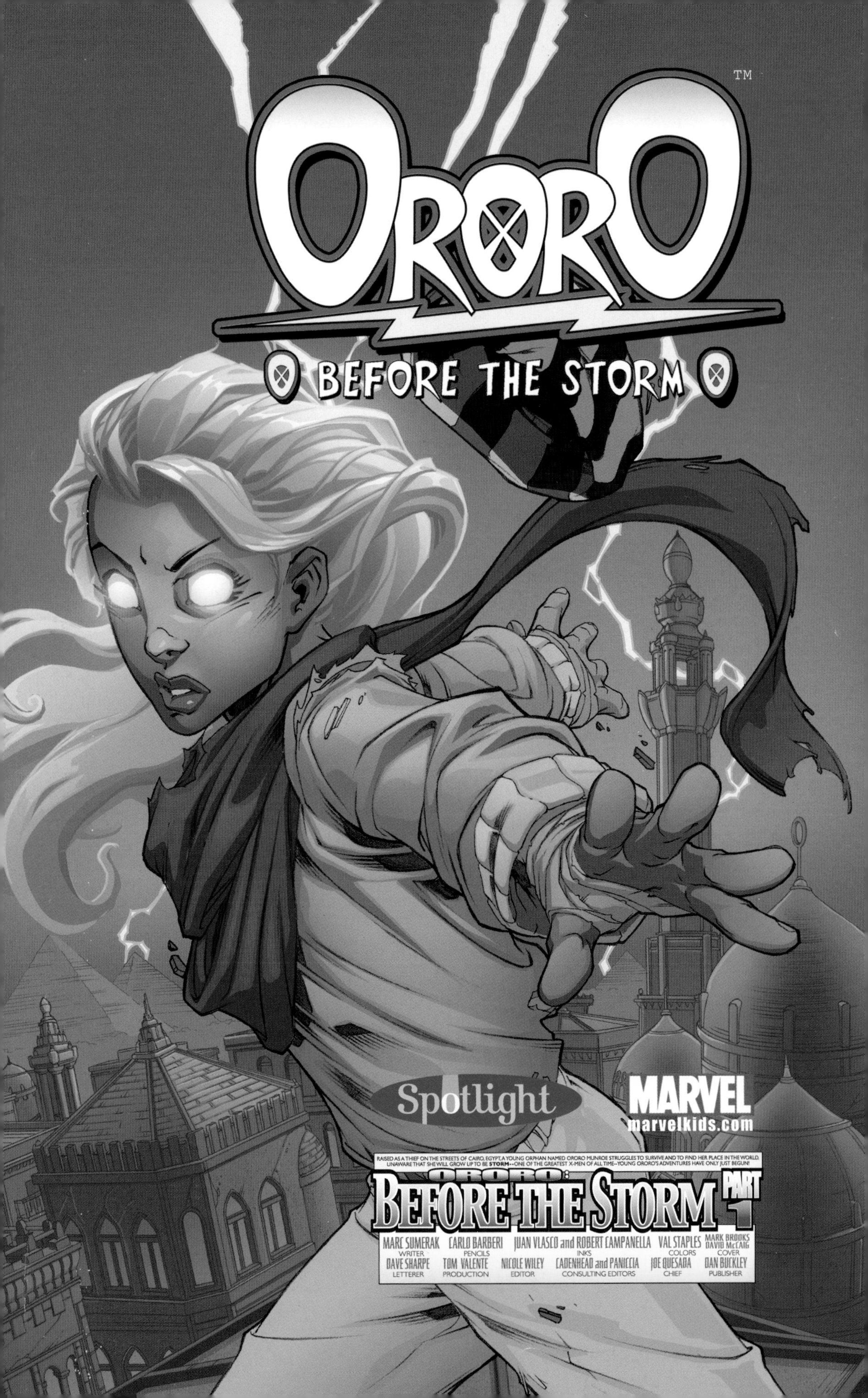

ORORO™
BEFORE THE STORM
Spotlight
MARVEL
marvelkids.com
RAISED AS A THIEF ON THE STREETS OF CAIRO, EGYPT, A YOUNG ORPHAN NAMED ORORO MUNROE STRUGGLES TO SURVIVE AND TO FIND HER PLACE IN THE WORLD. UNAWARE THAT SHE WILL GROW UP TO BE STORM--ONE OF THE GREATEST X-MEN OF ALL TIME--YOUNG ORORO'S ADVENTURES HAVE ONLY JUST BEGUN!
ORORO: BEFORE THE STORM PART 1
MARC SUMERAK WRITER
CARLO BARBERI PENCILS
JUAN VLASCO and ROBERT CAMPANELLA INKS
VAL STAPLES COLORS
MARK BROOKS DAVID McCAIG COVER
DAVE SHARPE LETTERER
TOM VALENTE PRODUCTION
NICOLE WILEY EDITOR
CADENHEAD and PANICCIA CONSULTING EDITORS
JOE QUESADA CHIEF
DAN BUCKLEY PUBLISHER

visit us at www.abdopublishing.com

Reinforced library bound edition published in 2013 by Spotlight, a division of the ABDO Group, 8000 West 78th Street, Edina, Minnesota 55439. Spotlight produces high-quality reinforced library bound editions for schools and libraries. Published by agreement with Marvel Entertainment, LLC. The stories, characters, and incidents mentioned are entirely fictional. All rights reserved. Used under authorization.

Printed in the United States of America, North Mankato, Minnesota.
052012
092012
♻This book contains at least 10% recycled materials.

TM & © 2012 Marvel & Subs.

Library of Congress Cataloging-in-Publication Data

Sumerak, Marc.
   Ororo : before the Storm / story by Marc Sumerak ; art by Carlo Barberi. -- Reinforced library bound ed.
      <v. 1-> cm. -- (Ororo)
   "Marvel."
   Summary: Long before she became the X-Man known as Storm, a young orphan named Ororo Munroe stalks the streets of Cairo, stealing under the tutelage of Achmed El-Gibar and yearning for the greatness her mother knew she would find.
   ISBN 978-1-61479-024-2 (part 1) -- ISBN 978-1-61479-025-9 (part 2) -- ISBN 978-1-61479-026-6 (part 3) -- ISBN 978-1-61479-027-3 (part 4)
   1. Graphic novels. [1. Graphic novels. 2. Superheroes--Fiction. 3. Orphans--Fiction. 4. Robbers and outlaws--Fiction. 5. Cairo (Egypt)--Fiction. 6. Egypt--Fiction.] I. Barberi, Carlo, ill. II. Title.
   PZ7.7.S86Oro 2012
   741.5'973--dc23
                                        2012000932

ISBN 978-1-61479-024-2 (reinforced library edition)

All Spotlight books are reinforced library binding and manufactured in the United States of America.

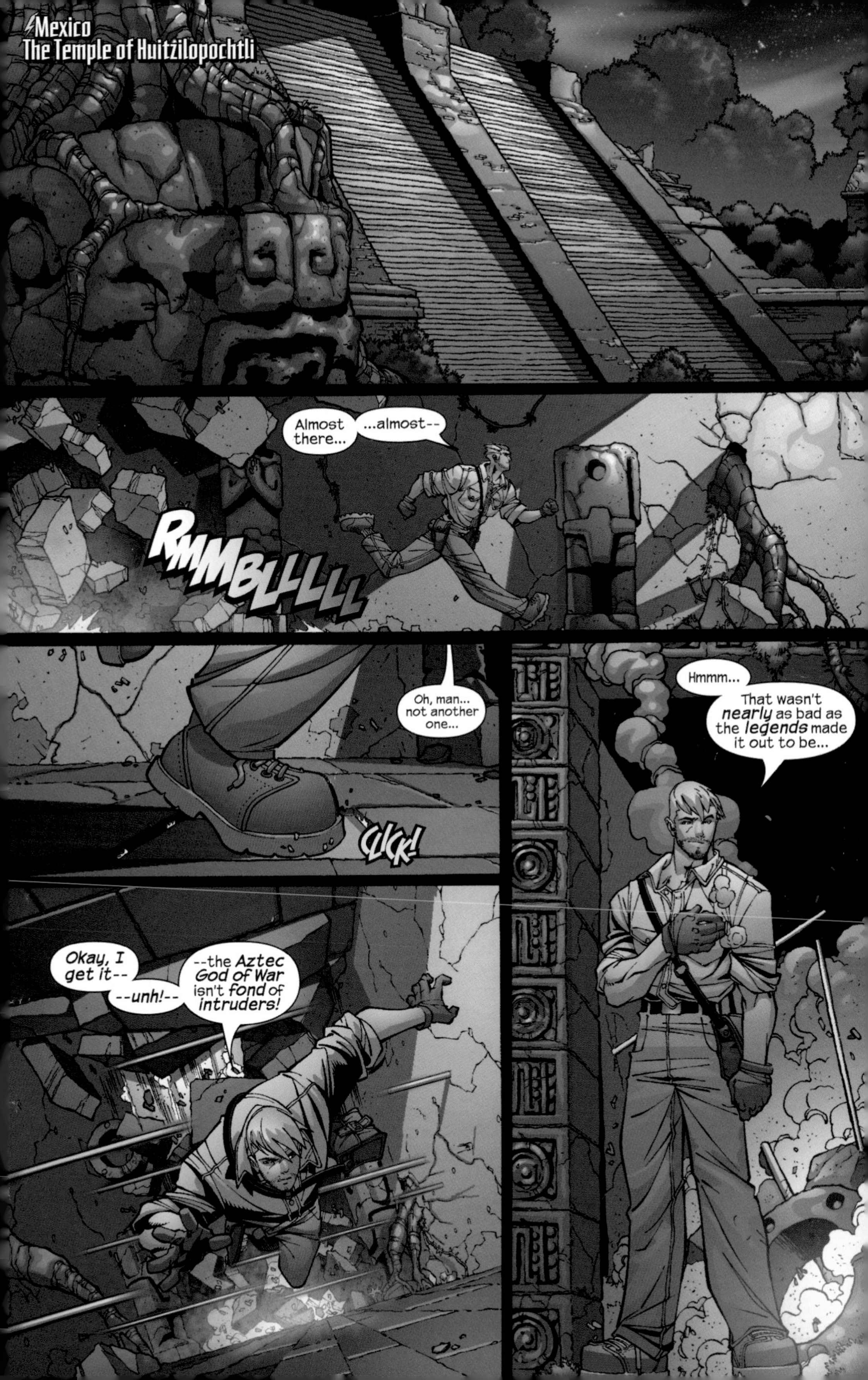
Mexico
The Temple of Huitzilopochtli
Almost there...
...almost--
RMMBLLLLL
Oh, man... not another one...
CLICK!
Okay, I get it--
--unh!--
--the Aztec God of War isn't fond of intruders!
Hmmm...
That wasn't nearly as bad as the legends made it out to be...

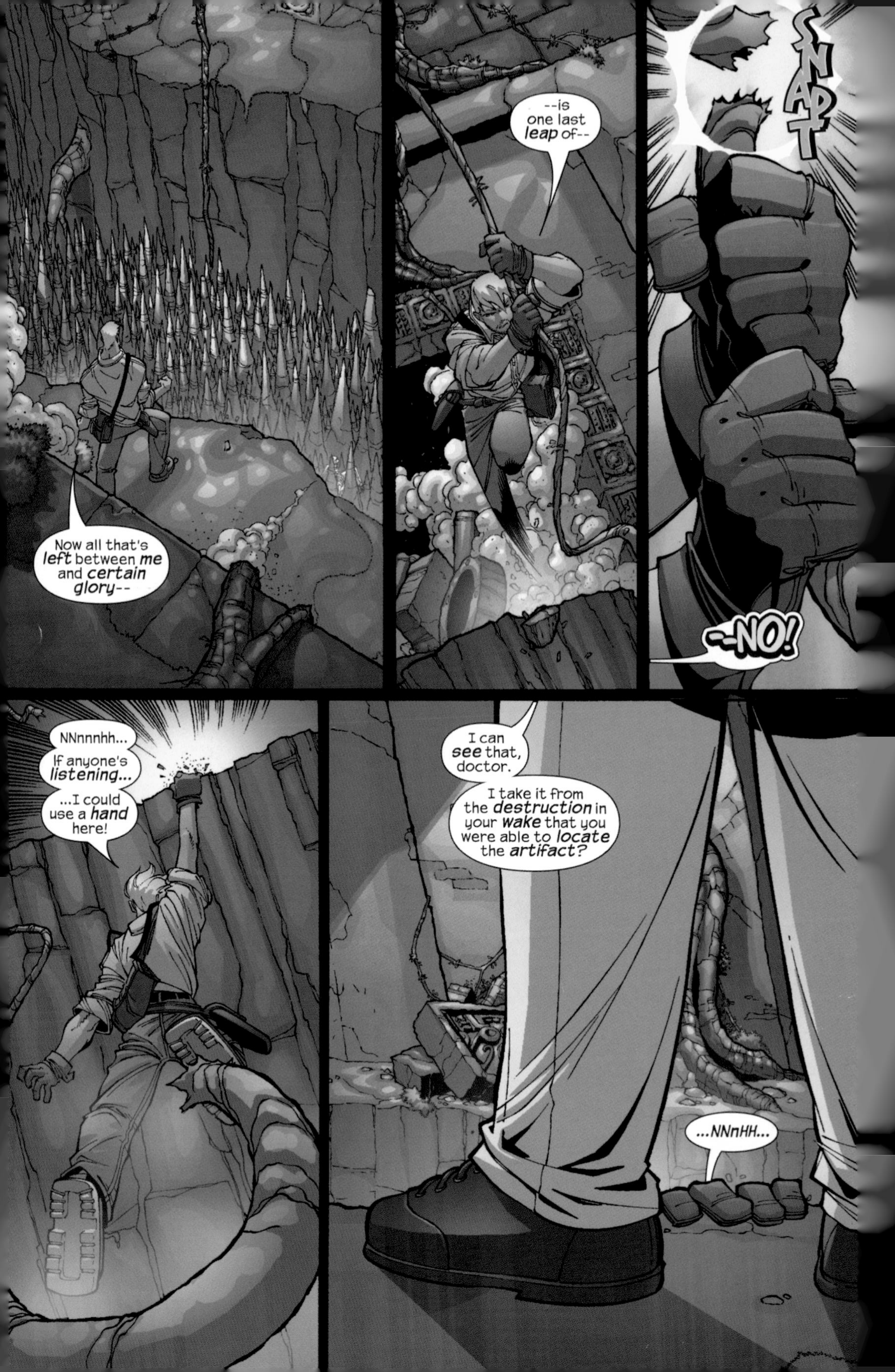
Now all that's left between me and certain glory--
--is one last leap of--
SNAP
--NO!
NNnnnhh...
If anyone's listening...
...I could use a hand here!
I can see that, doctor.
I take it from the destruction in your wake that you were able to locate the artifact?
...NNnHH...

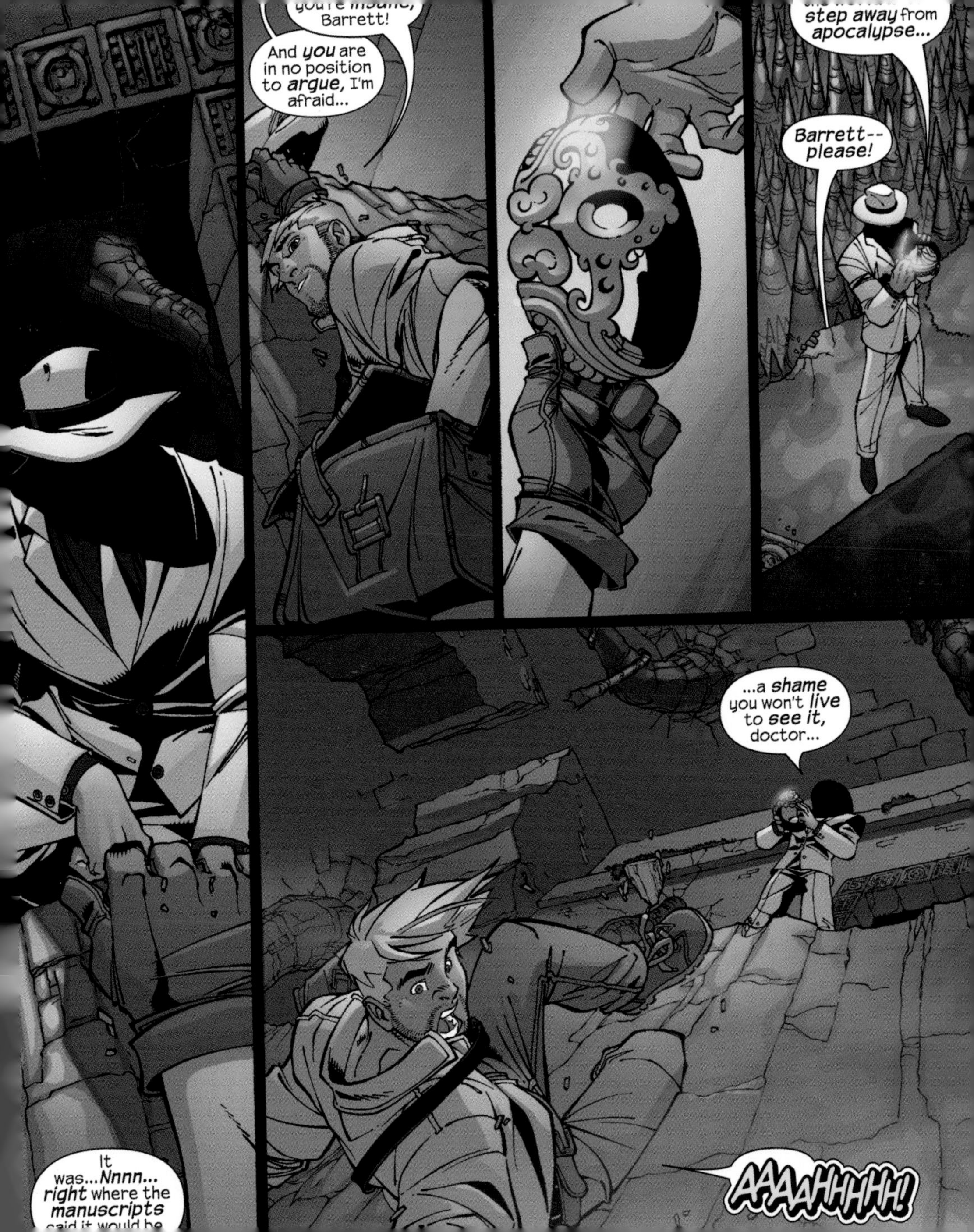

Barrett!
And you are in no position to argue, I'm afraid...
step away from apocalypse...
Barrett-- please!
...a shame you won't live to see it, doctor...
AAAAHHHHH!
It was...Nnnn... right where the manuscripts

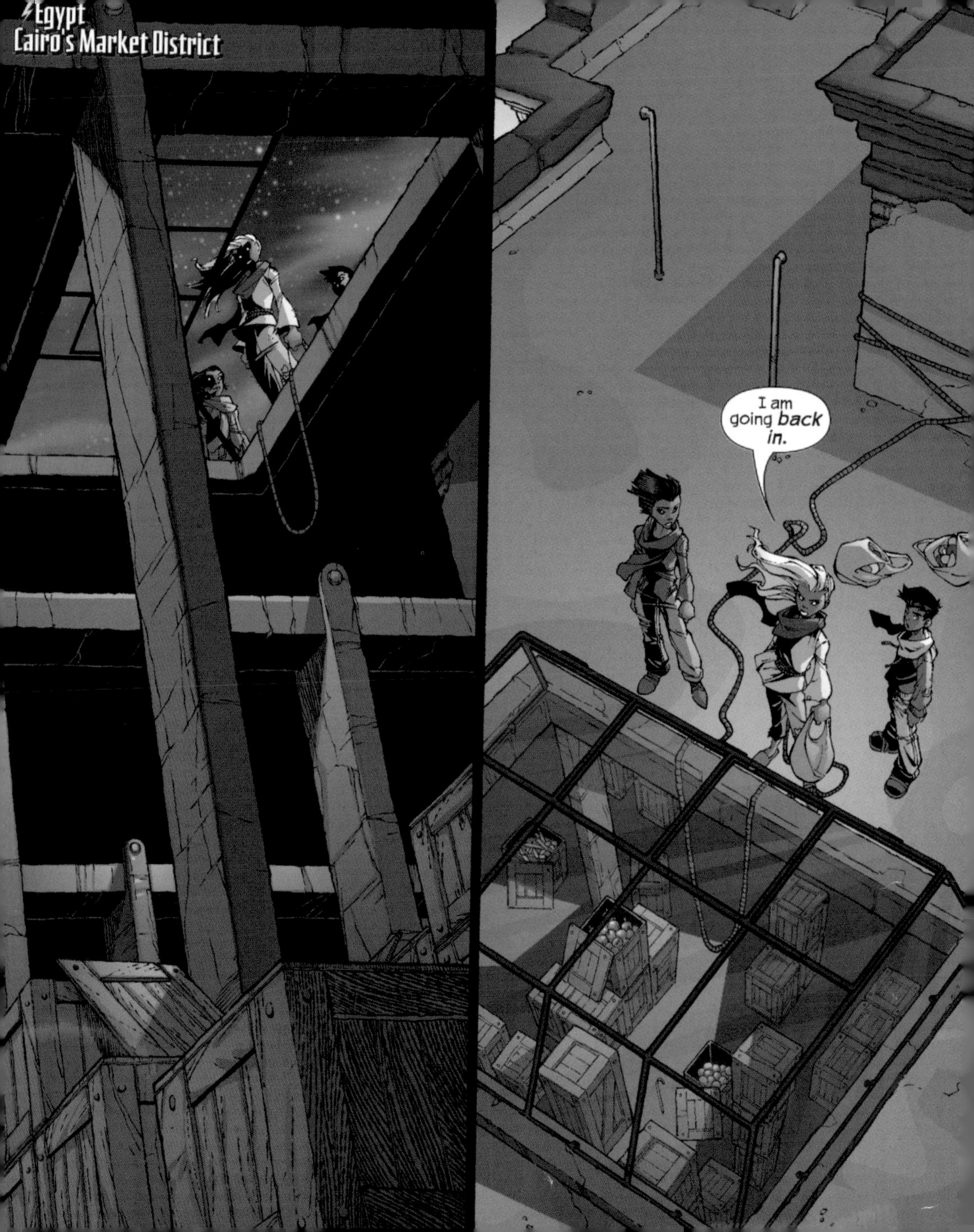
Egypt
Cairo's Market District
I am going back in.

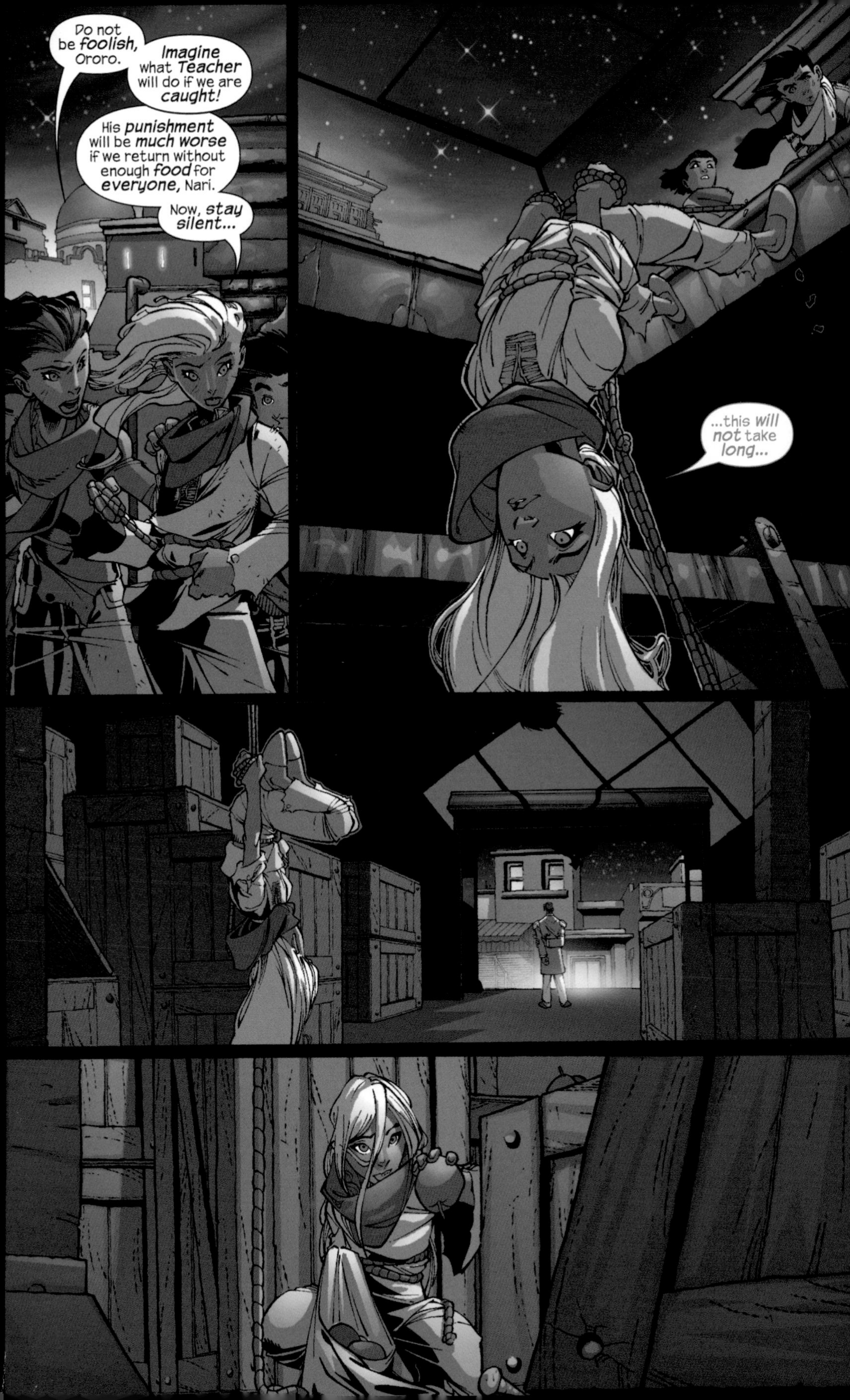

Do not be *foolish*, Ororo.
Imagine what *Teacher* will do if we are *caught!*
His *punishment* will be *much worse* if we return without enough *food* for *everyone*, Nari.
Now, *stay silent*...
...this *will not* take *long*...

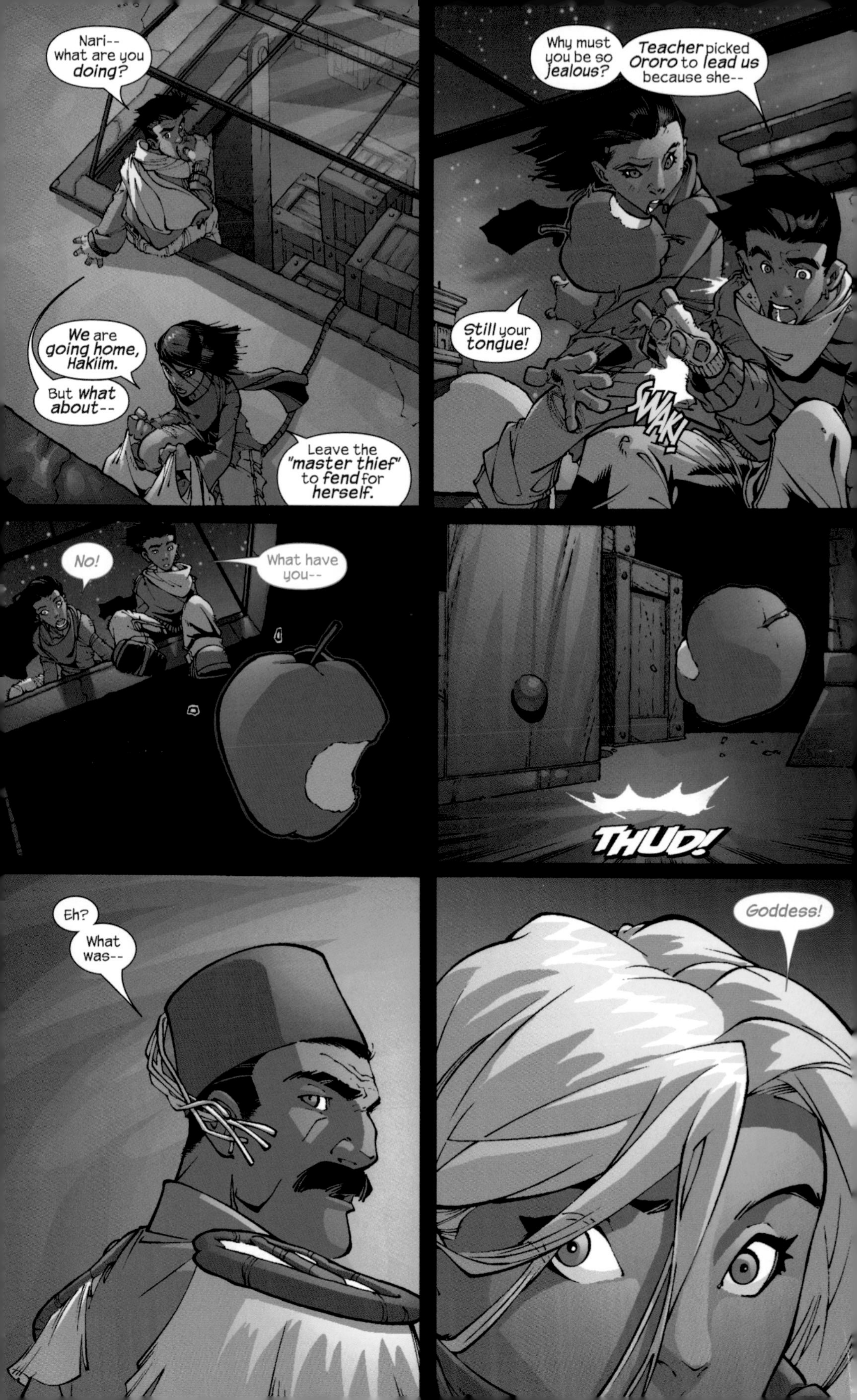
Nari-- what are you doing?
We are going home, Hakiim.
But what about--
Leave the "master thief" to fend for herself.
Why must you be so jealous?
Teacher picked Ororo to lead us because she--
Still your tongue!
SWAK!
No!
What have you--
THUD!
Eh? What was--
Goddess!

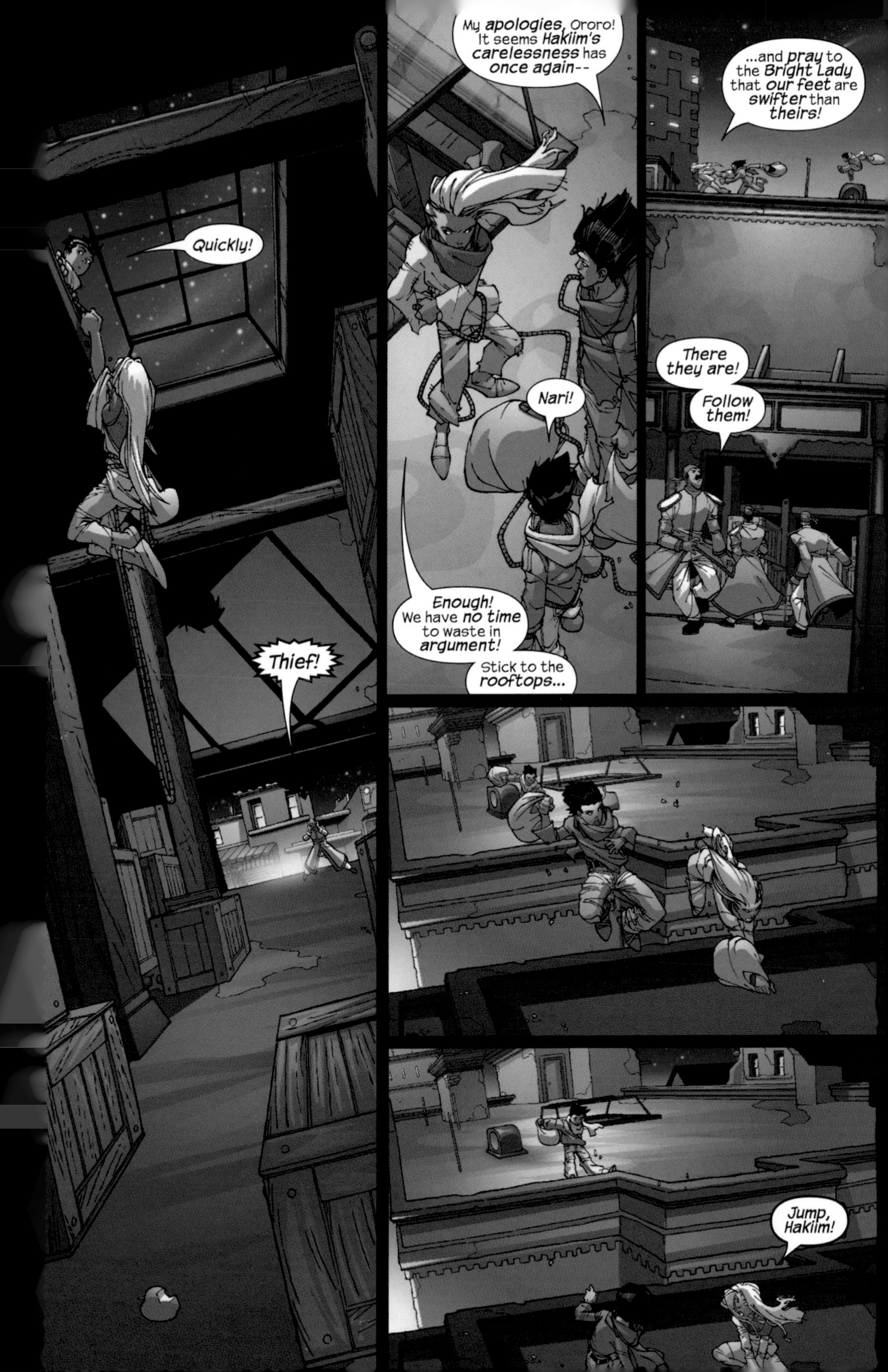
Quickly!
Thief!
My apologies, Ororo! It seems Hakiim's carelessness has once again--
Nari!
Enough! We have no time to waste in argument!
Stick to the rooftops...
...and pray to the Bright Lady that our feet are swifter than theirs!
There they are!
Follow them!
Jump, Hakiim!

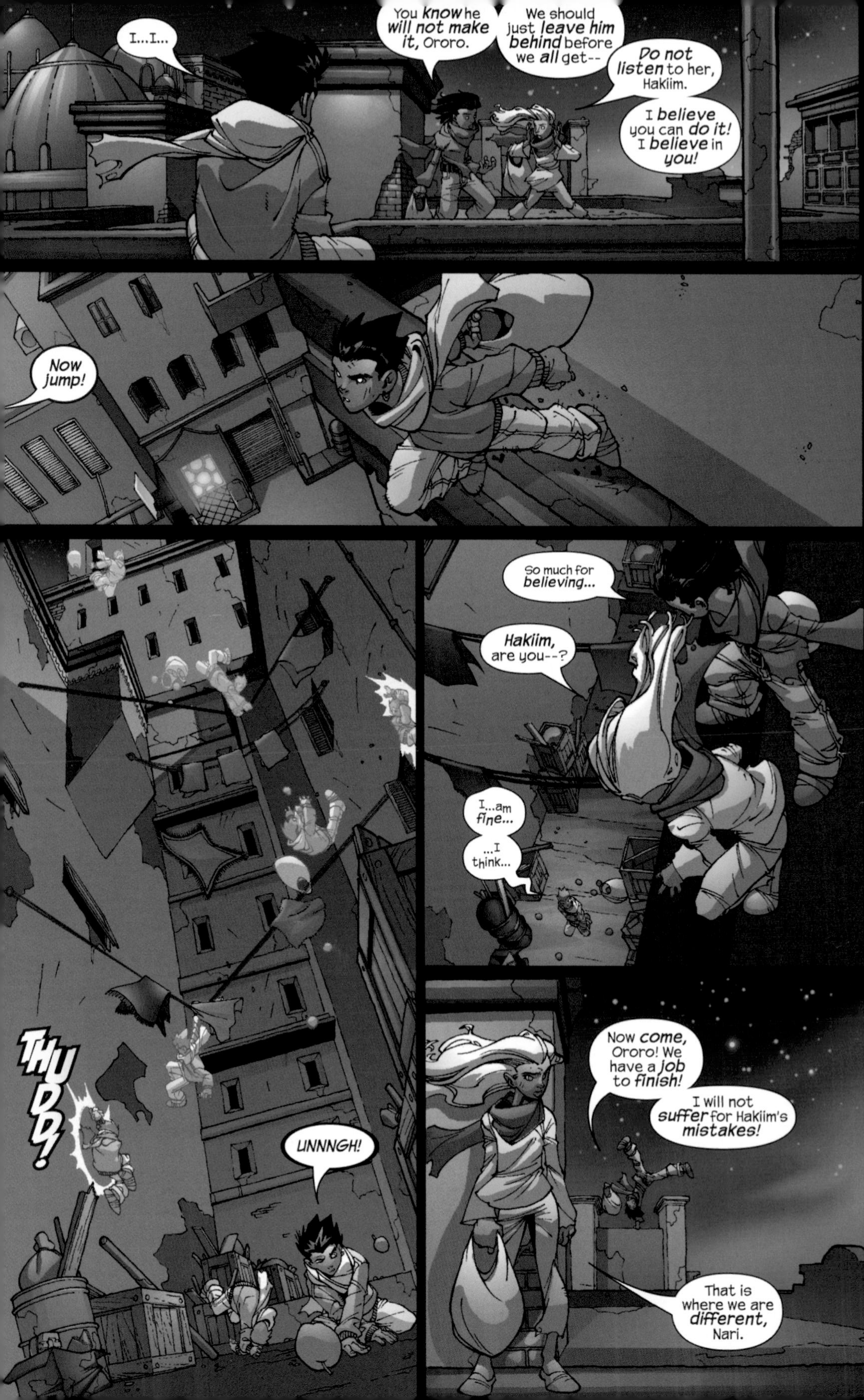
I...I...
You know he will not make it, Ororo.
We should just leave him behind before we all get--
Do not listen to her, Hakiim.
I believe you can do it! I believe in you!
Now jump!
THUDD!
UNNNGH!
So much for believing...
Hakiim, are you--?
I...am fine...
...I think...
Now come, Ororo! We have a job to finish!
I will not suffer for Hakiim's mistakes!
That is where we are different, Nari.

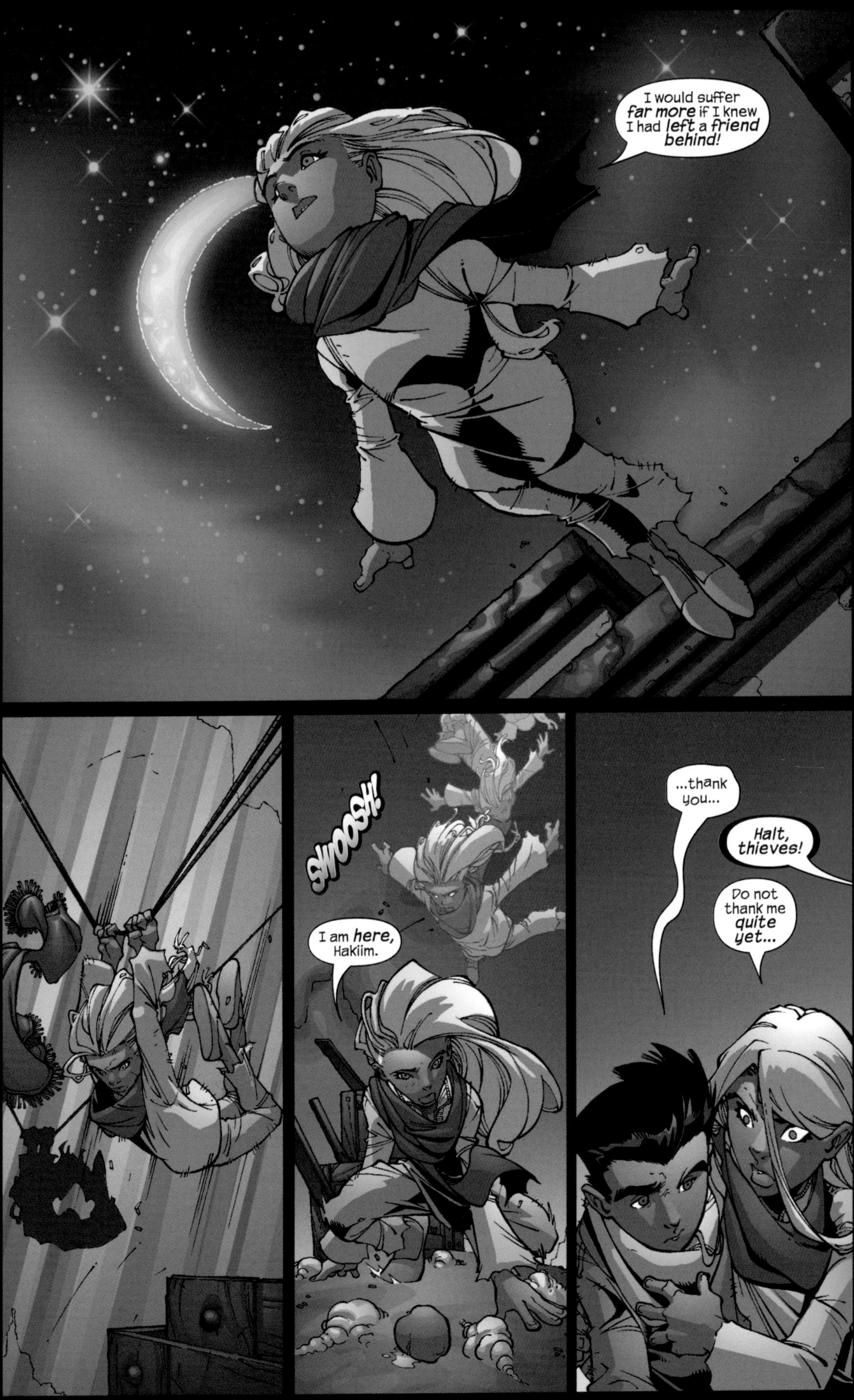
I would suffer *far more* if I knew I had *left* a *friend behind!*
SWOOSH!
I am *here,* Hakiim.
...thank you...
Halt, thieves!
Do not thank me *quite yet...*

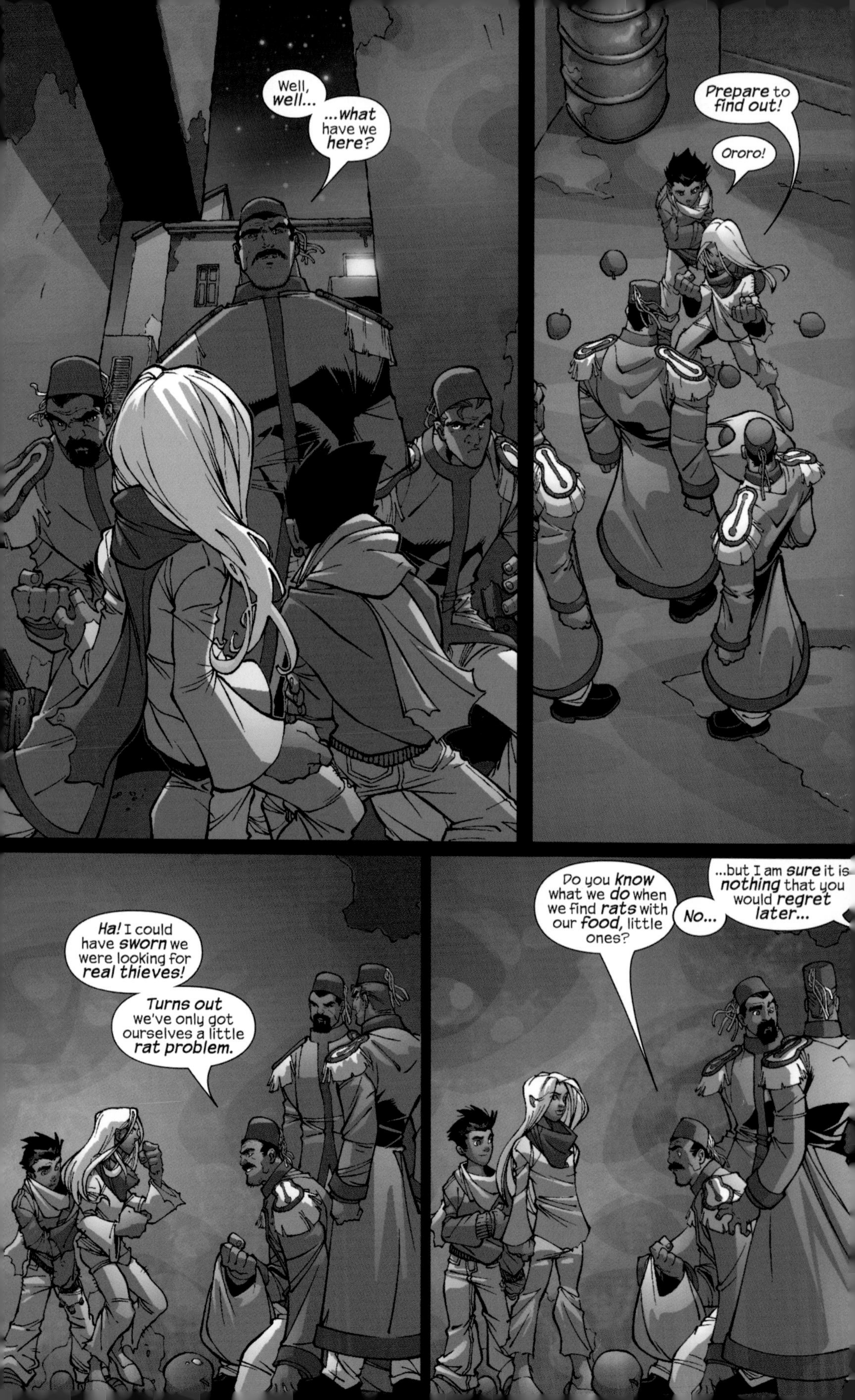
Well, well...
...what have we here?
Prepare to find out!
Ororo!
Ha! I could have sworn we were looking for real thieves!
Turns out we've only got ourselves a little rat problem.
Do you know what we do when we find rats with our food, little ones?
No...
...but I am sure it is nothing that you would regret later...

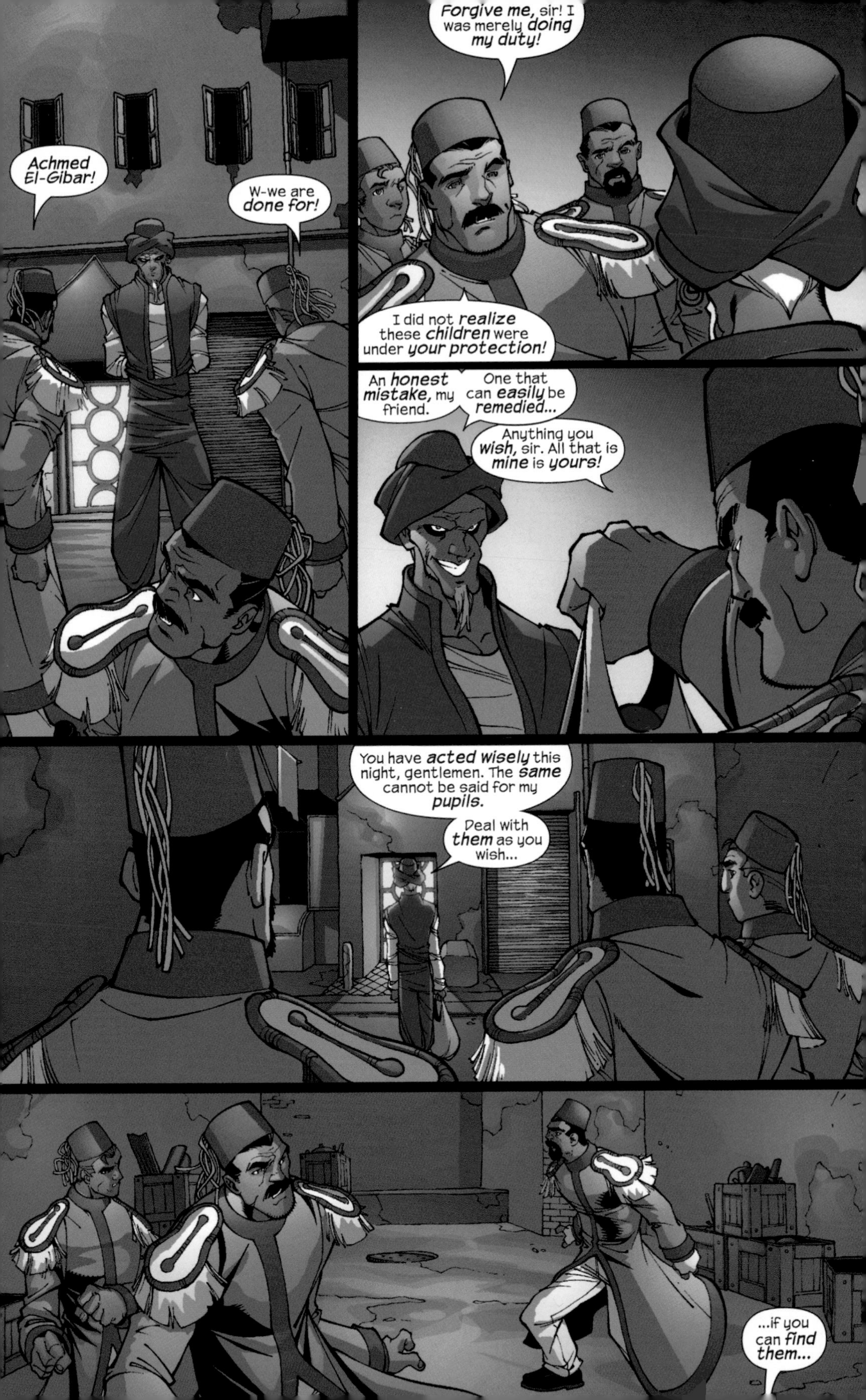
Achmed El-Gibar!
W-we are done for!
Forgive me, sir! I was merely doing my duty!
I did not realize these children were under your protection!
An honest mistake, my friend.
One that can easily be remedied...
Anything you wish, sir. All that is mine is yours!
You have acted wisely this night, gentlemen. The same cannot be said for my pupils.
Deal with them as you wish...
...if you can find them...

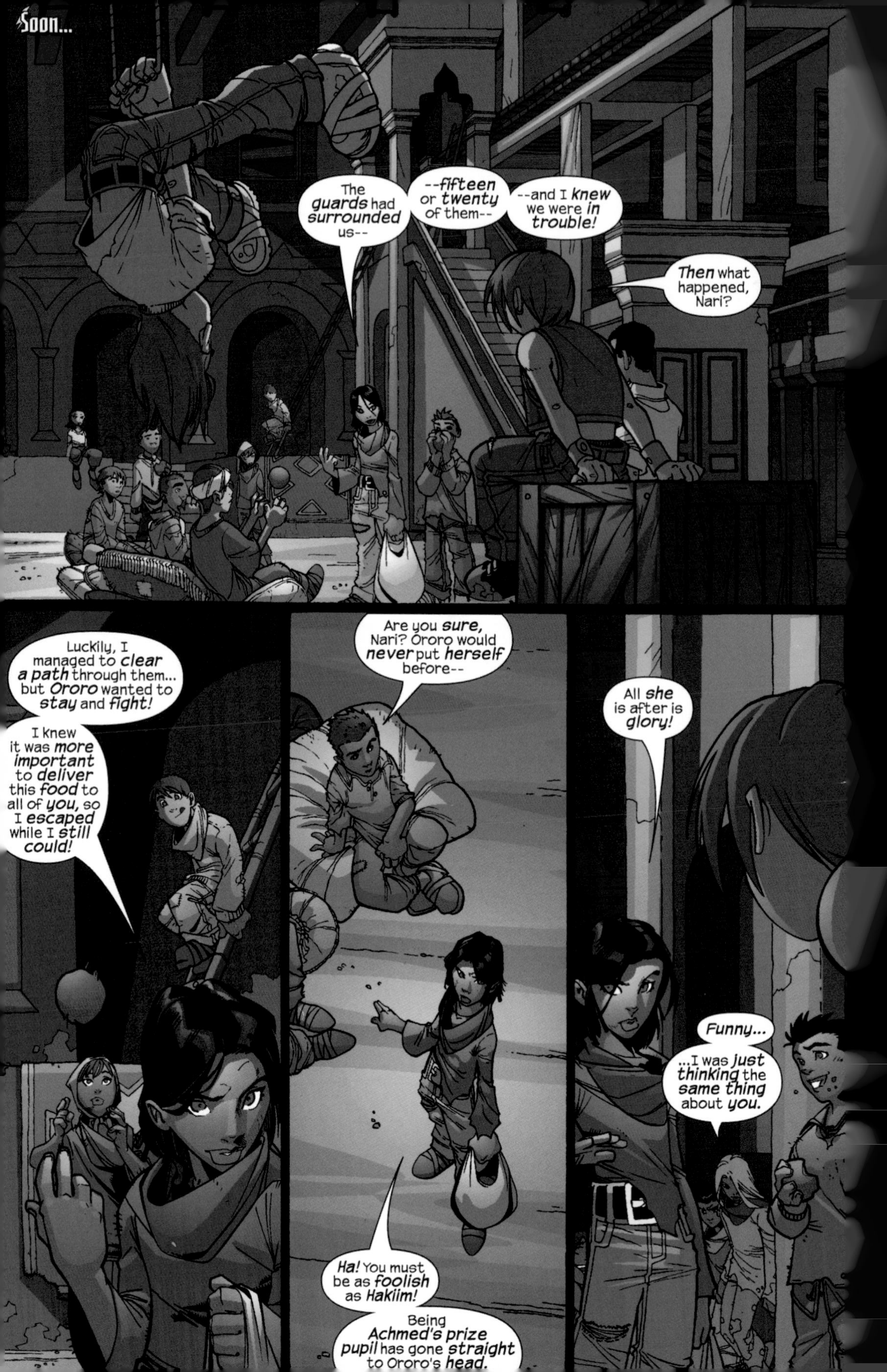
Soon...
The guards had surrounded us--
--fifteen or twenty of them--
--and I knew we were in trouble!
Then what happened, Nari?
Luckily, I managed to clear a path through them... but Ororo wanted to stay and fight!
I knew it was more important to deliver this food to all of you, so I escaped while I still could!
Are you sure, Nari? Ororo would never put herself before--
Ha! You must be as foolish as Hakiim!
Being Achmed's prize pupil has gone straight to Ororo's head.
All she is after is glory!
Funny...
...I was just thinking the same thing about you.

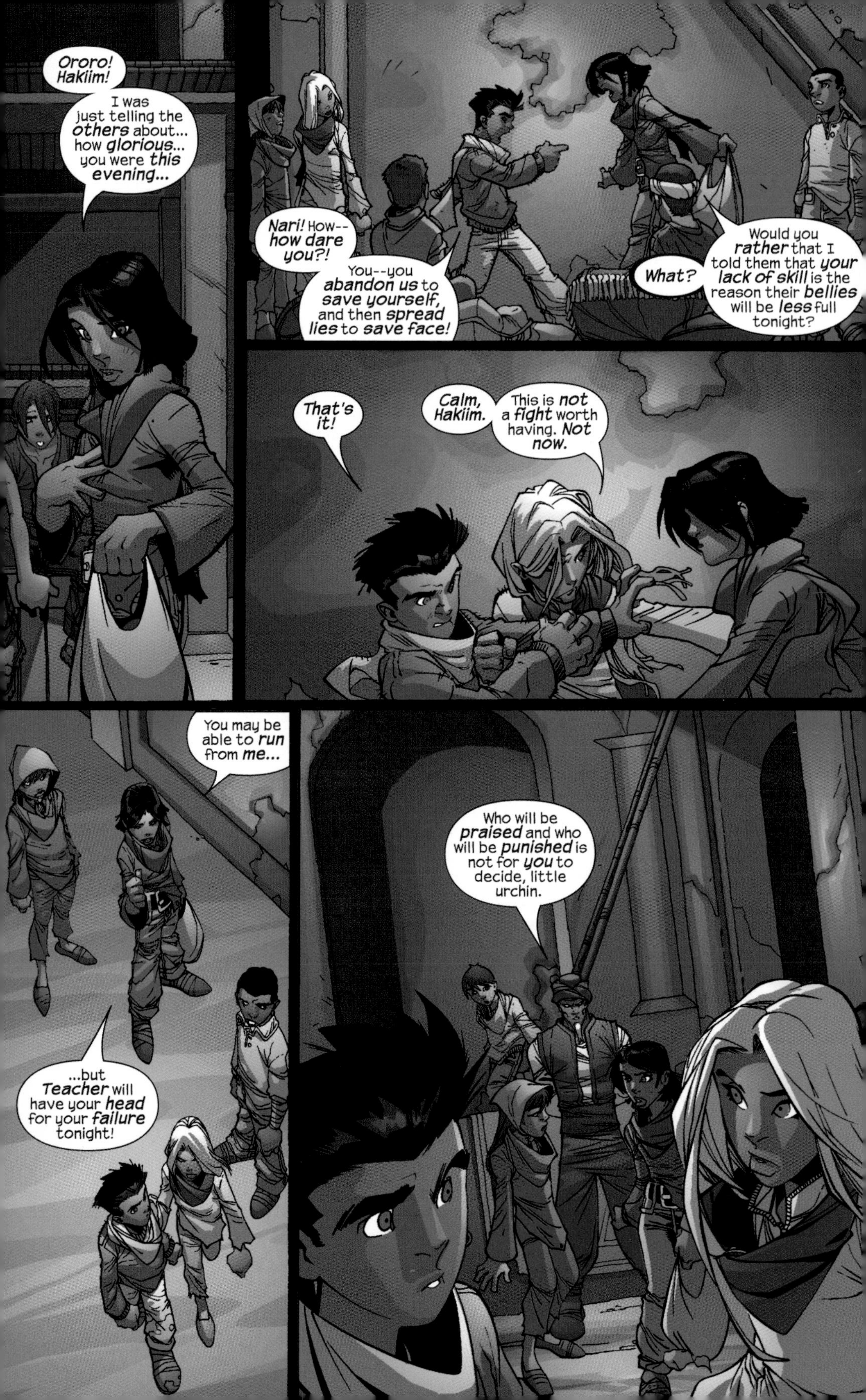
Ororo! Hakiim!
I was just telling the others about... how glorious... you were this evening...
Nari! How--how dare you?!
You--you abandon us to save yourself, and then spread lies to save face!
What?
Would you rather that I told them that your lack of skill is the reason their bellies will be less full tonight?
That's it!
Calm, Hakiim.
This is not a fight worth having. Not now.
You may be able to run from me...
...but Teacher will have your head for your failure tonight!
Who will be praised and who will be punished is not for you to decide, little urchin.

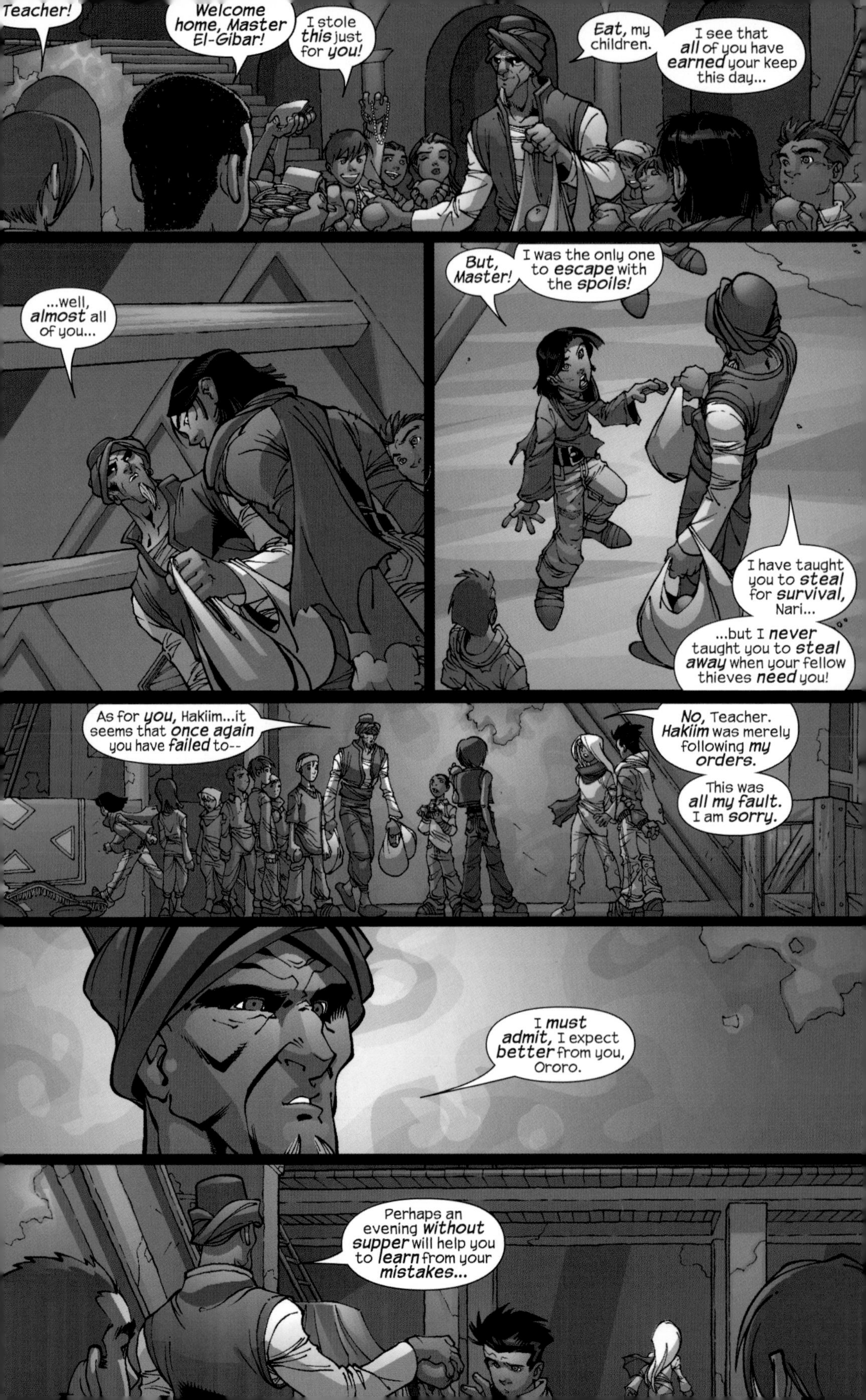
Teacher!
Welcome home, Master El-Gibar!
I stole this just for you!
Eat, my children.
I see that all of you have earned your keep this day...
...well, almost all of you...
But, Master!
I was the only one to escape with the spoils!
I have taught you to steal for survival, Nari...
...but I never taught you to steal away when your fellow thieves need you!
As for you, Hakiim...it seems that once again you have failed to--
No, Teacher. Hakiim was merely following my orders.
This was all my fault. I am sorry.
I must admit, I expect better from you, Ororo.
Perhaps an evening without supper will help you to learn from your mistakes...

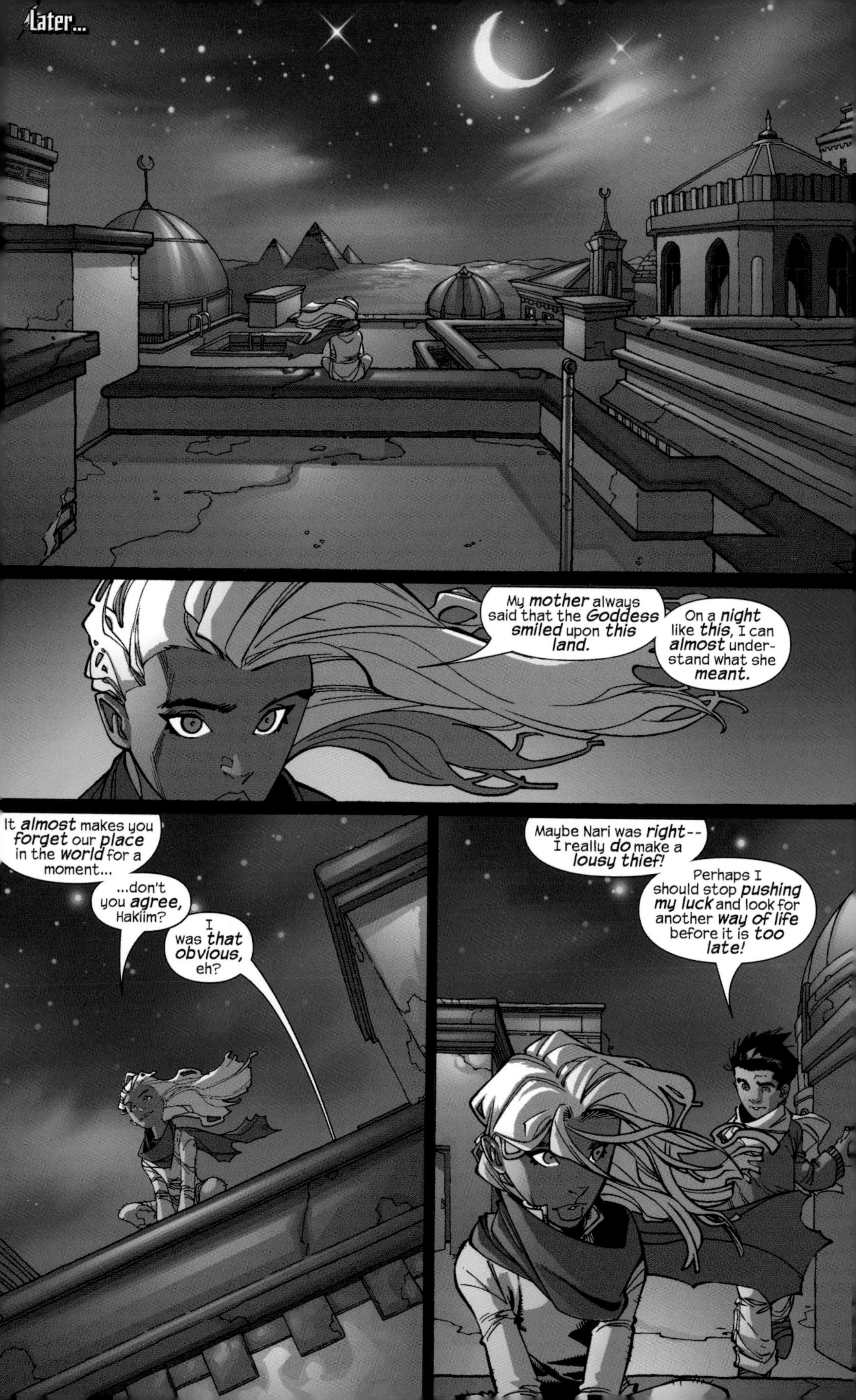
Later...
My mother always said that the Goddess smiled upon this land.
On a night like this, I can almost understand what she meant.
It almost makes you forget our place in the world for a moment...
...don't you agree, Hakiim?
I was that obvious, eh?
Maybe Nari was right-- I really do make a lousy thief!
Perhaps I should stop pushing my luck and look for another way of life before it is too late!

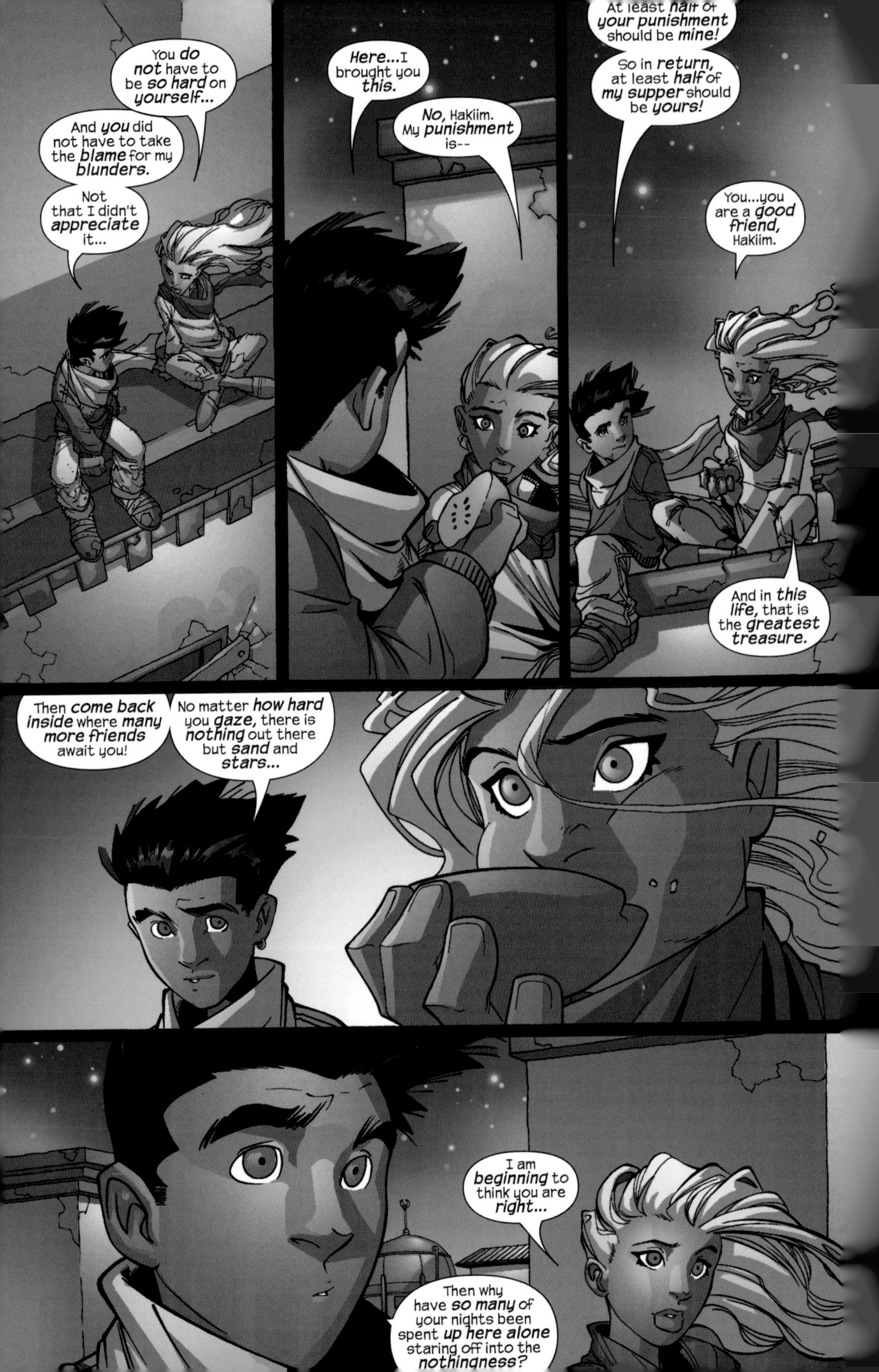

You do not have to be so hard on yourself...
And you did not have to take the blame for my blunders.
Not that I didn't appreciate it...
Here...I brought you this.
No, Hakiim. My punishment is--
At least half of your punishment should be mine!
So in return, at least half of my supper should be yours!
You...you are a good friend, Hakiim.
And in this life, that is the greatest treasure.
Then come back inside where many more friends await you!
No matter how hard you gaze, there is nothing out there but sand and stars...
I am beginning to think you are right...
Then why have so many of your nights been spent up here alone staring off into the nothingness?

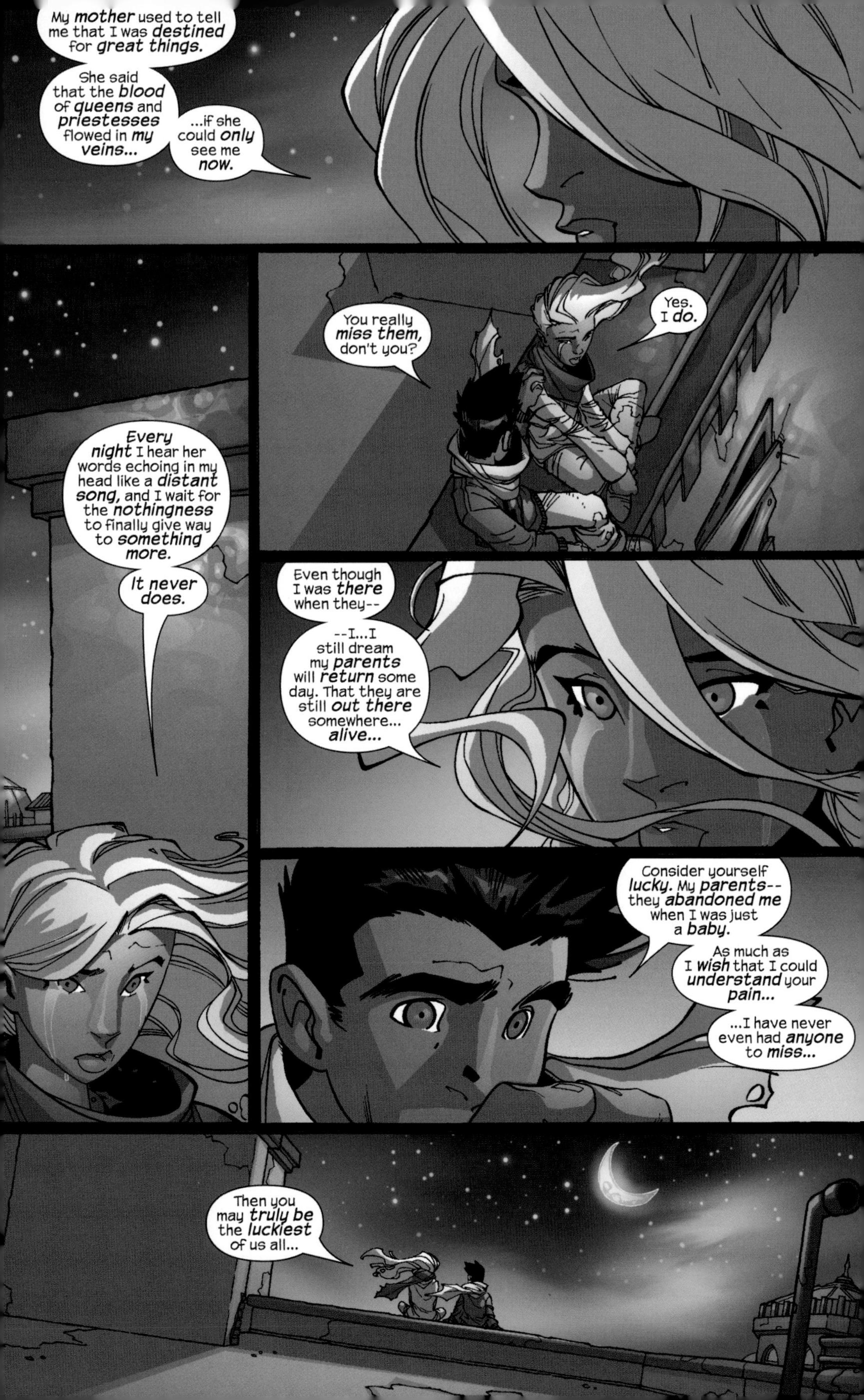
My mother used to tell me that I was destined for great things.
She said that the blood of queens and priestesses flowed in my veins...
...if she could only see me now.
Every night I hear her words echoing in my head like a distant song, and I wait for the nothingness to finally give way to something more.
It never does.
You really miss them, don't you?
Yes. I do.
Even though I was there when they--
--I...I still dream my parents will return some day. That they are still out there somewhere... alive...
Consider yourself lucky. My parents--they abandoned me when I was just a baby.
As much as I wish that I could understand your pain...
...I have never even had anyone to miss...
Then you may truly be the luckiest of us all...

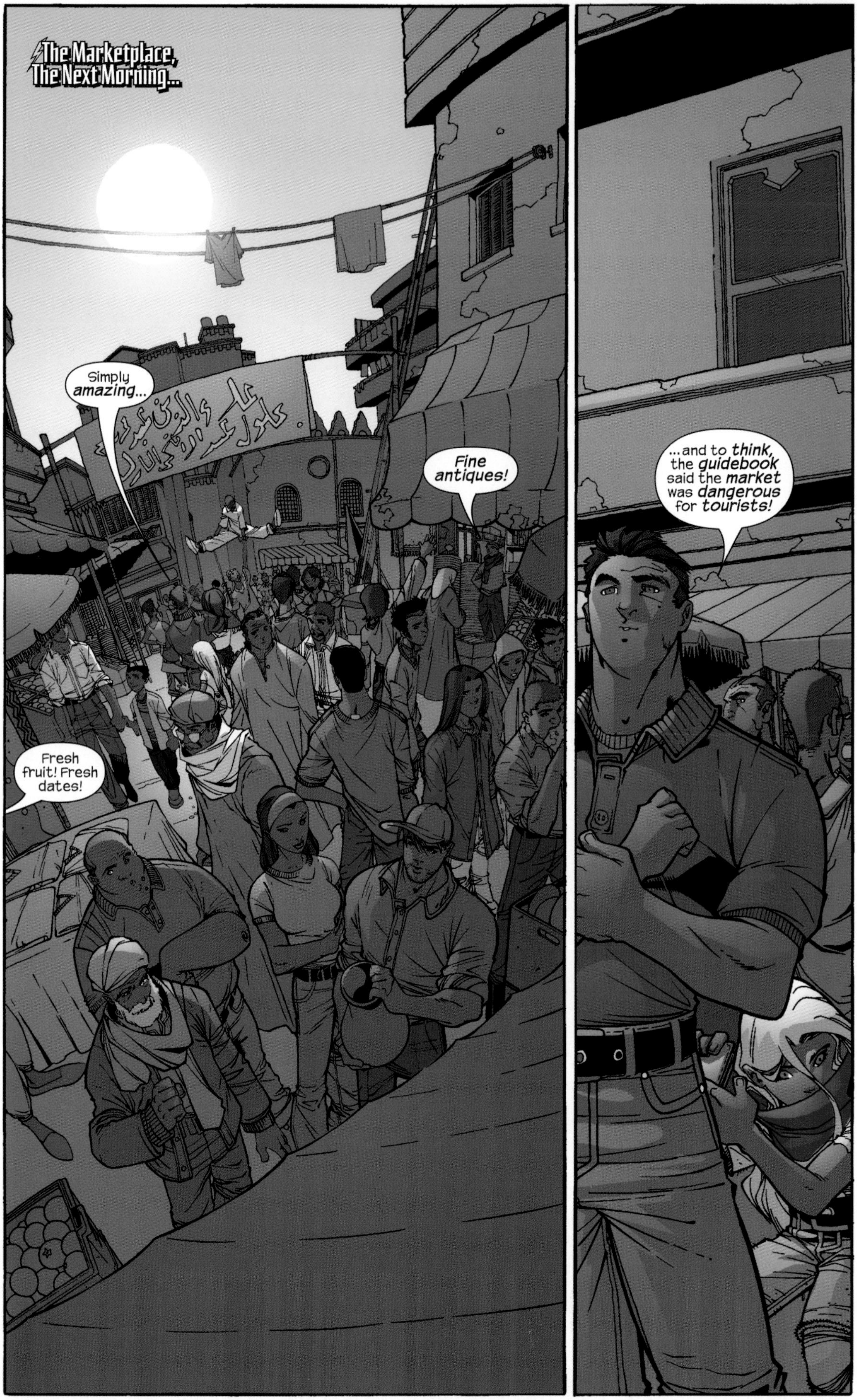
The Marketplace, The Next Morning...
Simply amazing...
Fine antiques!
Fresh fruit! Fresh dates!
...and to think, the guidebook said the market was dangerous for tourists!

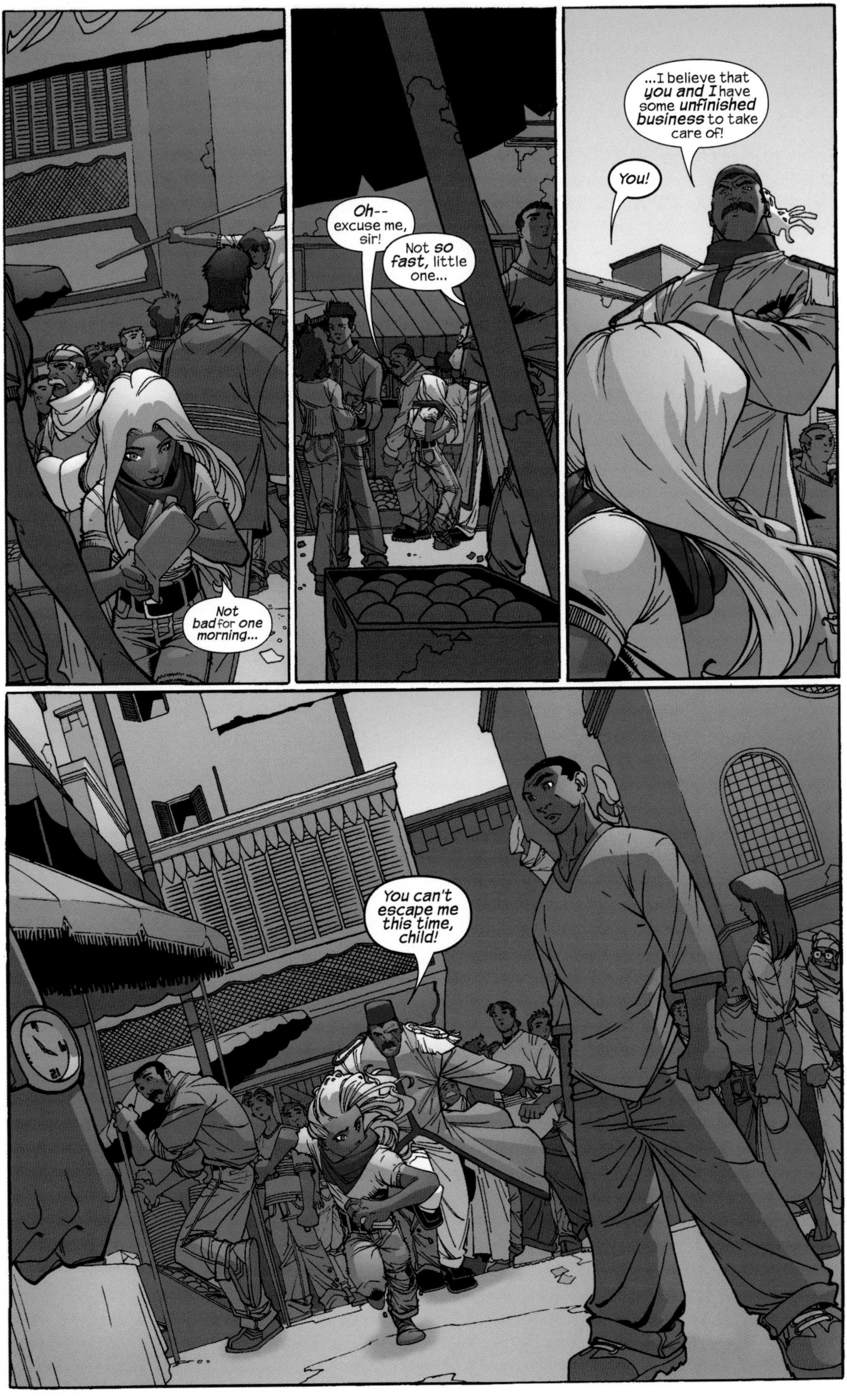
Not bad for one morning...
Oh-- excuse me, sir!
Not so fast, little one...
...I believe that you and I have some unfinished business to take care of!
You!
You can't escape me this time, child!

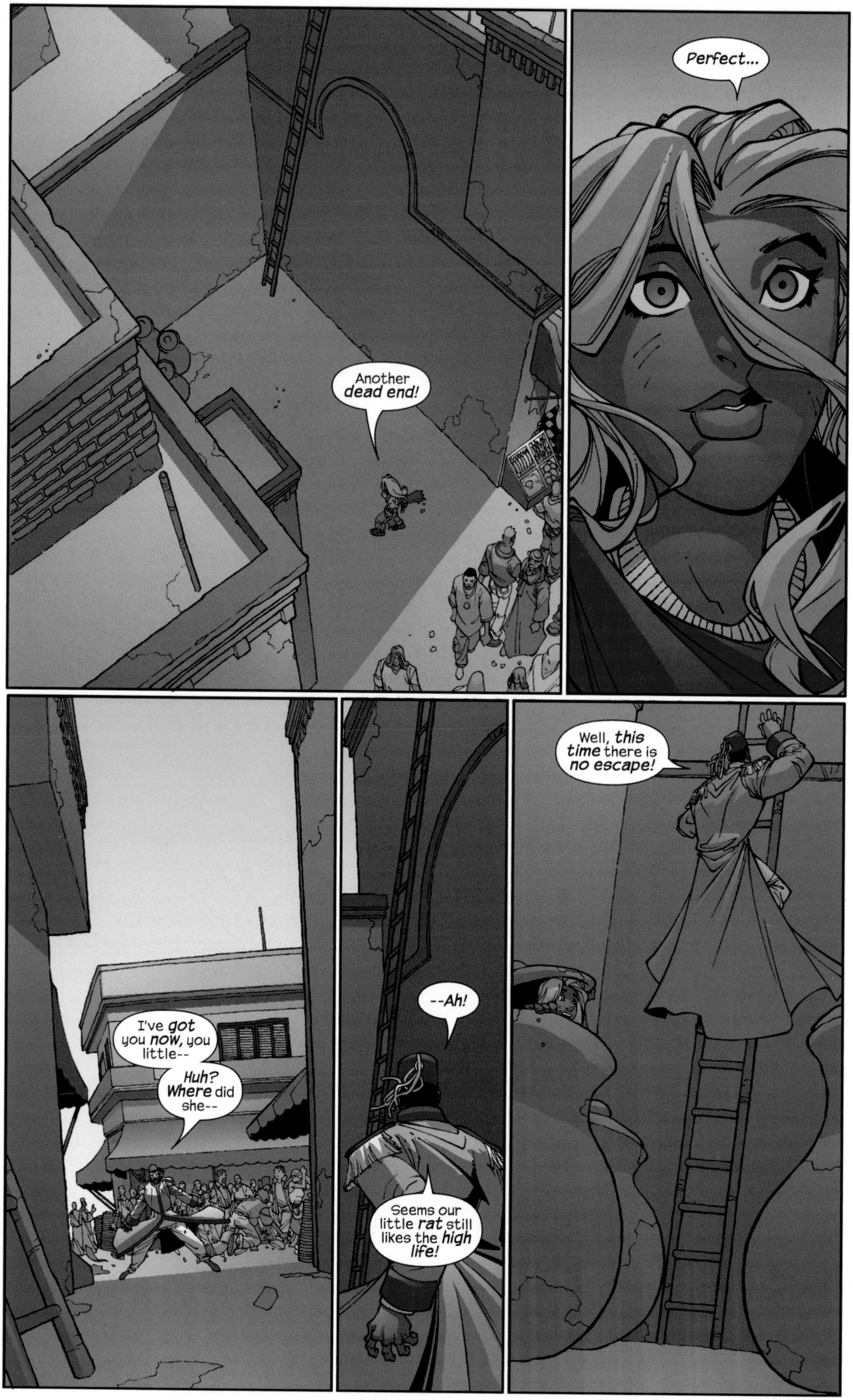
Another dead end!
Perfect...
I've got you now, you little--
Huh? Where did she--
--Ah!
Seems our little rat still likes the high life!
Well, this time there is no escape!

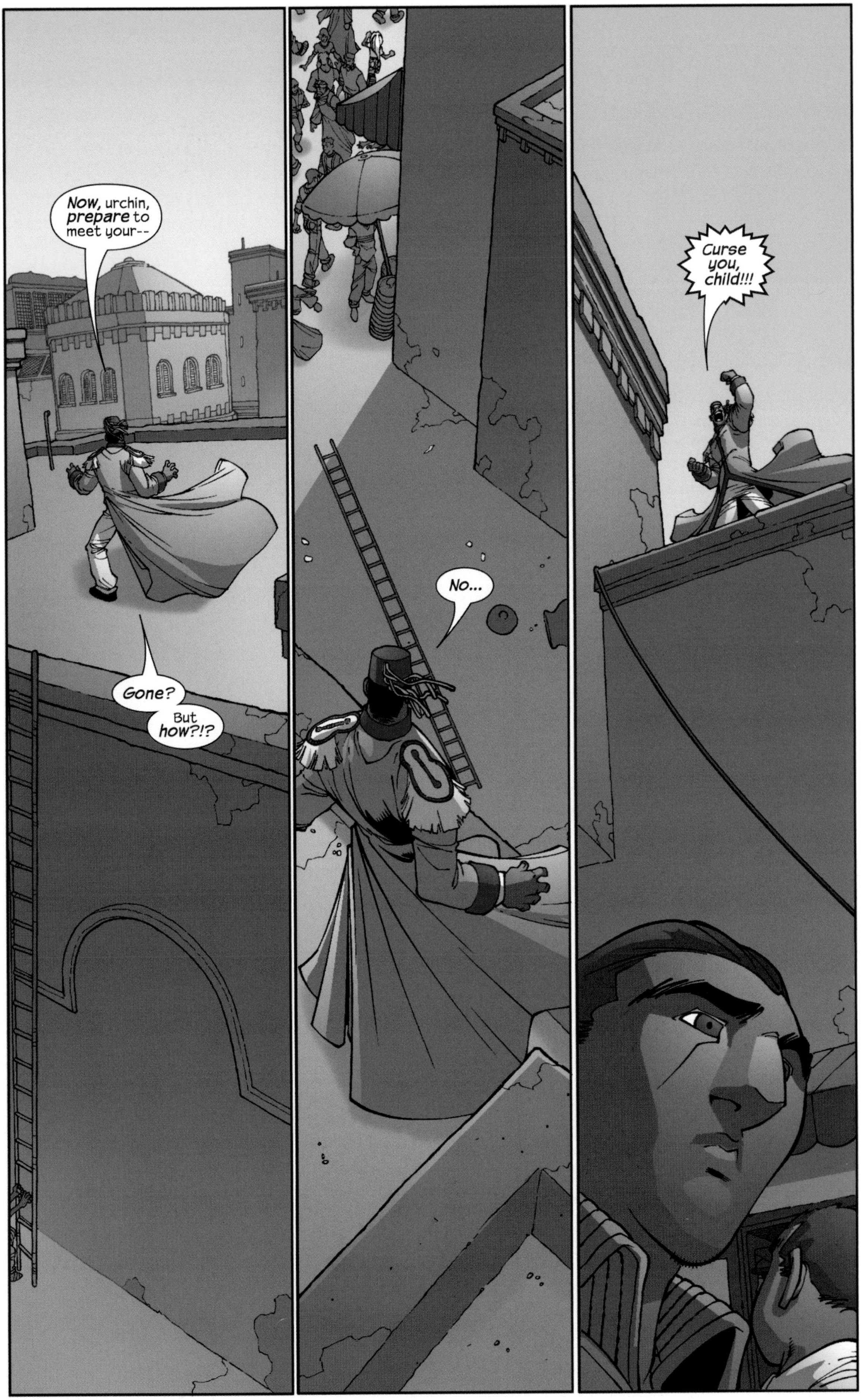
Now, urchin, prepare to meet your--
Gone?
But how?!?
No...
Curse you, child!!!

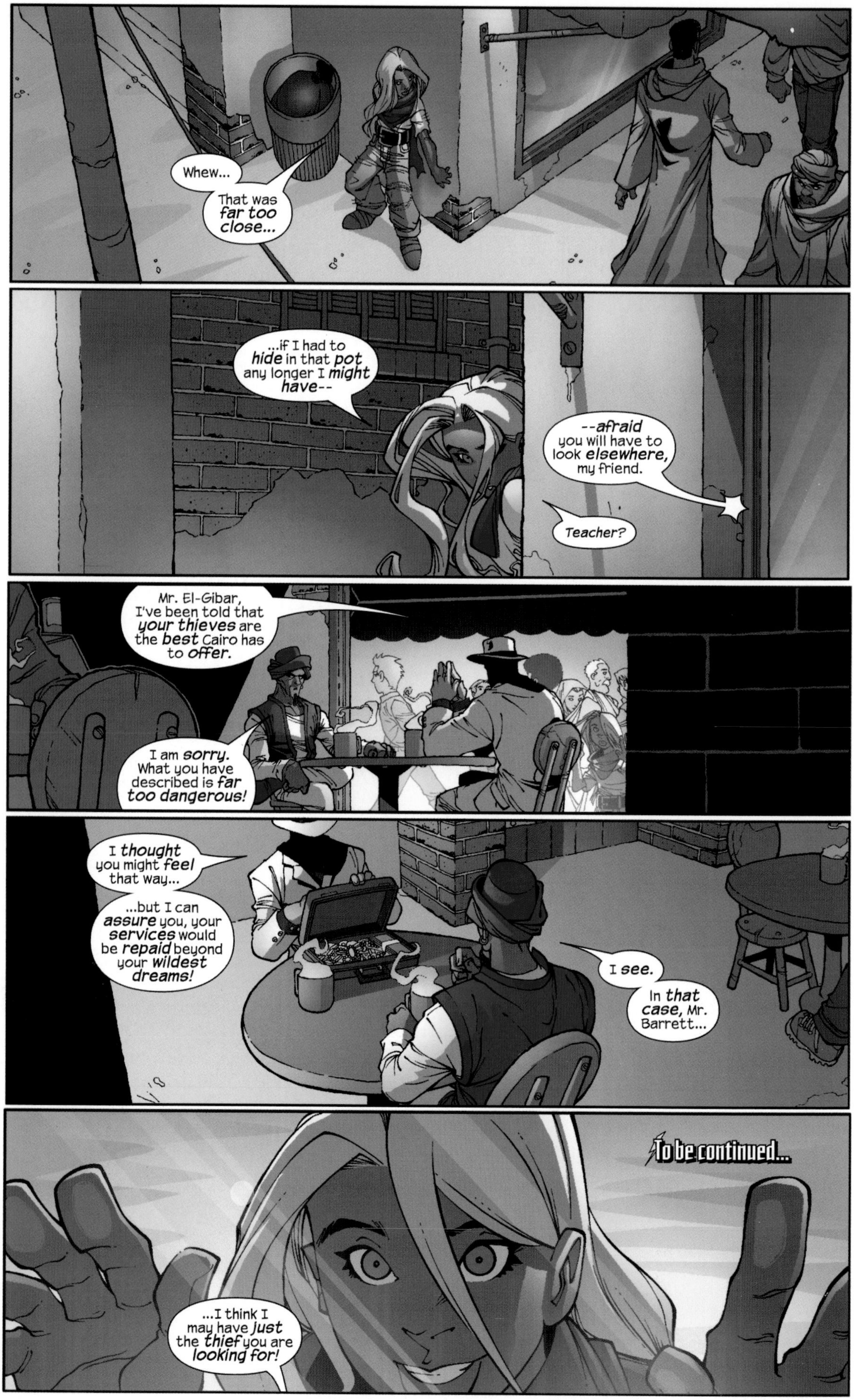
Whew...
That was far too close...
...if I had to hide in that pot any longer I might have--
--afraid you will have to look elsewhere, my friend.
Teacher?
Mr. El-Gibar, I've been told that your thieves are the best Cairo has to offer.
I am sorry. What you have described is far too dangerous!
I thought you might feel that way...
...but I can assure you, your services would be repaid beyond your wildest dreams!
I see.
In that case, Mr. Barrett...
To be continued...
...I think I may have just the thief you are looking for!